HERO`S

To order additional copies of this book, contact:
Xlibris
844-714-8691
www.Xlibris.com
Orders@Xlibris.com

ISBN: Softcover   978-1-6641-9026-9
        EBook   978-1-6641-9025-2

Print information available on the last page

Rev. date: 08/25/2021

HERO`S

BY: JACK R. DOWLER SR.

DEDICATION

This story is dedicated to all veterans, men and women, past, present and future, for serving our country. A few hero's in my family:

♦:♦   Nancy Dowler - U.S. Army

♦:♦   Duane Blackmon - U.S. Air Force

♦:♦   Jack Reisinger- U.S. Army- MIA

♦:♦   Glenn Dowler - U.S. Army- KIA

♦:♦   Robert Dowler - U.S. Arm·y,- KIA

I personally thank you all and may God bless each and every one of you.

Jack R. Dowler Sr.

HERO'S

This story is about three old vets: Jack, Pete and Dan. They were all in the Vietnam War together but that was the one thing they never talked about. They would meet once, sometimes twice a week at their favorite place to eat, a small restaurant named Sara's. It was named after the lady who ran the place.

The men loved to give her a hard time, but she didn't mind. She just gave them a hard time right back. Jack liked to call her "Princess" because he knew that her father named her that because "Sara" means "Princess", but Jack was the only one that could get away with it. He used to have a crush on her in high school but when "Uncle Sam" called him off to war - well - when he came back, things we different. Not bad, not good, not s re how, but different. Jack rode an old Harley Chopper. He called it "Traveler" because of all the miles that he put on it. Pete rode an Indian with all the fringe and tassels. He just loved that look. He called it "Chief" because Pete says "It just fits". Both men argued all the time that his bike was better than the other.

Dan rode a trike that he called "Black Widow". He said he "Just liked the name." The only thing the three men agreed on was, motorcycles should be black and chrome!

Dan just could not hold up two wheels anymore. He was looking rough very thin. The doctors said he had that cancer beat once, but it came back and was taking a toll on him. Dan was a fighter though, you got to give him that. He would not give up easily. They all had breakfast at Sara's and went for their ride. Little did they know, it would be their last ride together- all three of them together. It was a week later, and it was a beautiful morning. The sun was bright and warm, Jack was the first to arrive at Sara' s.

He was just sitting there drinking his coffee, thinking about what a nice ride Pete, Dan and he would have today. After they ate of course. Jack looks up at Sara and says "Where are they? I'm getting hungry". Sara replied "Be patient you old fart. They will be here in no time". Just then, Pete walks in with his head down. He continues walking over to the table where Jack is sitting, not saying a word, he didn't have to. Jack and Sara knew...Dan was gone. Jack looks at Pete and asks " When?" Pete looks at Jack with tears in his eyes and a lump in his throat "Just a couple hours ago. About 6am." Jack slowly stands up and walks towards the door.

"Where are you going?" Pete says, "To fulfill my promise" Jack replied. Jack turns towards the door to leave, Pete yells "Jack! Not without me you're not!" Jack just gives him a thumbs up and walks out the door. Jack has a flash back to when they were younger, walking through the jungles of Vietnam.

- Dan: "Jack, make me a promise."

- Jack: "What's that?"

- D- "When I die, cremate my body and put my ashes in the Gulf of Mexico."

- J- "You're not going die."

- D- "I will someday, sometime, promise me please."

- J- "I promise if you don't shut up, I will flush you down the john."

- Dan stops, "Jack, I mean this. This is important to me. You are all I have."

- Jack looks Dan right in the eyes and says "Don't worry brother. You have my word."

Three days later, Jack and Pete pull up in front of Sara's. While they start to walk in and Pete says, "Let's eat so we can hit the road." They sit down at their normal table, a young lady that they have never seen before walks up to them. "Hello, my name is Ann. I will be your waitress today. May I take your order?"

Jack and Pete just stare at each other for a moment. Jack says "Ok, who are you and where is the Princess?" "The Princess?" Ann replies cocking her head to one side, looking at Jack oddly. Jack says "Sara, where's Sara?" Ann looks at him for a moment longer before replying "Oh...I'm Sara's niece and she said she had to go out of town for a week or two. I'm running the place 'till she gets back. Something about a death in the family but no one I know." Jack and Pete stare at each other, Jack says "Oh no, oh no, no, no!" they both stand up and head towards the door. When it opens, there is Sara sitting on Dan's bike "Black Widow".

Pete says, "What are you..." and before he could get another word out, Sara interrupt's him and says "It was in his will. Besides, you didn't think after all this time you boys were going without me, did ya? By the way Jack, we are going through states with helmet laws, so you better have a "real" helmet." Jack replies slightly sarcastically "Princess, first of all, I have a "real" helmet on my bike. Now let's get something straight right now...you may run that restaurant, and you do a great job doing it, but you do not run me or this trip. Do you understand?" "Oh, yes sir!" Sara replied smiling from ear to ear (she gives a small salute as she's smiling). She looks at Pete, winks and says, "I love a man that takes control." Pete's trying hard not to laugh. Jack puts his head down and rubs his forehead. " I think I'm getting a headache." "Let's go inside and get some breakfast and coffee...I know how you two are and you need to eat before we hit the road. Besides I need to make sure Ann has everything under control while I'm gone" Sara says turning between Jack and Pete. They all head back into the restaurant, place their orders and chow down as quickly as they can so they can hit the road. Sara finish's squaring up things with Ann before giving her a hug saying "I'll be back soon. Thank you for taking care of the place for me while I'm gone." Ann looks at Sara with a warm smile on her face "Just be careful."

Jack, Pete and Sara are riding down the road, the sun is shining bright and it's warm. The trees are so green and you can smell the freshly cut grass in the air. Dan would love this, Jack thought to himself. If there was such a thing as a perfect day (weather wise- of course), this is it. The miles go by quickly. Pete points at his gas tank. It's time to get gas. It's also a good time to stretch our legs and walk around a little. The three of them pull up to the gas pumps and fill their tanks. Jack and Pete are ready to go, but they are waiting on Sara. She is looking at herself in the side mirror of Black Widow fixing her makeup. Pete looks at Jack, "How long did you say this trip was going to take?" "It depends on how many times, we have to stop so Princess can fix her makeup." Jack said to Pete. Sara jumps right in, not missing a beat "Not as many times as we have to stop so you two can take a leak." She winks at them, smiling. They all laugh and jump on their bikes. Heading down the road again, the view keeps getting better and better, or they were just seeing things like they've never seen them before. It's almost like they are seeing nature for the first time.

All of a sudden, Jack pulls ahead and stays to the right of the road. He puts his left foot out to point at a dead skunk in the road. The song " Dead Skunk" pops into Jack's head...he starts singing to himself "...Dead skunk in the middle of the road and he's stinkin' to high heaven." Pete does the same, staying close to the right side of the road, putting his left foot out to let Sara know about the dead skunk. Sara stays to the right as much as she can, but the left rear tire of Black Widow hits the dead skunk. A few miles down the road, they pull into a small diner, Jack and Pete park Traveler and Chief at one end of the parking lot and make Sara park Black Widow at the other end. As they were getting *off* of their bikes, a helicopter flies nearby. Jack falls on one knee by his bike, he has a flashback with military helicopters flying over.

Pete kneels beside Jack and puts his arm around his shoulder. "It's ok Jack. It's over." Pete says trying to help him as much as possible. Sara is looking out of the window inside the diner. You can see the concern on her face. She went inside to get a table for the three of them. She knew whatever made Jack fall was about the war. Pete would be a lot more help to Jack in this situation than she would be. But she wanted to be there for Jack as well. She was worried about him. She continues to watch on.

After a short time, Jack slowly stands and he and Pete start to walk inside to join Sara at the table, they find her at a booth. Once seated, Pete's quick to change the subject and start's going on and on about the dead skunk in the road. "I can't believe you hit that skunk!" Pete laughs. Sara replies "I couldn't help it, Black Widow is a little bit wider than Traveler and Chief." Pete chuckles "That's for sure." Sara glanced at Pete "What's that supposed to mean?" Jack jumps in quickly "Hey, it's over, let's talk about something else while we eat before we hit the road."

They were finishing up when the old man running the place walks up and asks (in his southern accent) "Can I fill ya'lls drinks? How 'bout some dessert? We have the best apple pie in the county." Pete replies "No thanks, I think we're good." Jack was drinking the last of his coffee. The old man asks "If ya'll don't mind me askin', where ya heading?" Jack just wanted to say south and get out there as quickly as possible. But Pete had other plans, he proceeded to tell the old man the whole story, everything from the war to Dan being out on his bike and going to the Gulf. At the same time, Sara heads towards the jukebox and starts putting quarters into it. She makes her selection and walks over to Jack. "Come on, we have to dance, they are playing our song." Jack, looking very surprised says "We have a song? Since when?" "Of course, we do silly, well, at least we do now." Sara says, smiling. She grabs his hand, pulls him up and they dance. The song "Please Forgive Me" by Bryan Adam's is playing. When the song ends, Jack says "We really should get going." He looks at the old man and asks, "What do we owe you sir?" The old man looks at Jack and replies "You know, I lost a brother in Vietnam. Your money is no good here. Ya'll be safe and good luck." The three looked at each other before looking at the old man again. "Thank you" they said in unison. They left a tip and headed out the door. The old man yelled to them as they were leaving, "Ya'll welcome back here anytime!" A man in the next booth, who caught everything, looked up to the old man and said "Charlie, I think I have something to talk about in the morning." The man sitting in the booth was named Johnny, and he was a local talk show host.

The next morning, while on the air, Johnny tells everyone about the three's story and asks everyone listening, "...if you see these three people on motorcycles, just give them a wave and a little bit of encouragement". He encouraged all of his listeners to pass the word on about these three friends. Surprisingly, news traveled fast, and people did just what Johnny asked them to do. The next thing Jack, Pete and Sara knew, people were everywhere. People were on bridges and standing on the sides of the road. They were all waving flags and yelling encouraging words to them. It felt like there were people around every turn. Jack, Pete and Sara were shocked. They couldn't believe it, nor did they understand. They stopped to fill up and stretch when Sara says, "What in the world is going on around here?" Jack looks at her and replies "Looks like the story of our "little" trip got out." They both turn to Pete who shrugs. With a southern accent, Jack continues "...and it's movin' faster than gossip in a Baptist church!" Pete jumps in "Oh Lord, we have to get this man out of here. He starting to sound just like them!" They all start laughing. Just then, four young men walk up to them. They are on sport bikes and have a little attitude. One of them says "Look at what we have here guys, looks like some antiques and I don't mean the motorcycles." The four young men laugh. Pete's staring at them when he says, "Look son, why don't you get on your bike, take your friends with you and just head up the road." The young men turn to Pete then, the same one saying, "I'm not your son." Jack speaks up then, having enough already. "Yeah Pete, the kid's right. Our sons have more respect for their elders then these boys." The young man (he must be the "leader") turns to Jack and says, "Who are you calling boys, old man?" At the same time, he pokes Jack in the chest with his index finger. Jack grabs the young man's finger and pulls it back. The young man falls to his knees in pain.

The other young men start to move towards Jack. Pete puts his hand inside his vest like he's going to pull out a gun. Pete stares at the boys and says softly "I would not move any closer if I were you." Jack looks down at the young man and says "The last person to poke me in the chest went home with his finger in a pickle jar. Now, I am in a good mood today so if you apologize real nice to my friends and I, like I know you are going to, I will let you go home.... with your finger "attached." At first, the young man says nothing. Jack bends his finger back a little more. "Ok! Ok!" the young man cries out. "I'm sorry!" Jack looks down at the young man and says "Us old antiques can't hear so well anymore, what did you say? Again, and louder! I'm sorry what?" Jack barks. "I'm sorry sir! " the young man is actually crying now. His friends start backing away towards their bikes, Pete and Sara are standing there watching, trying so hard not to laugh at the current situation. Jack frowns at the young man and says "And young lady. I'm sorry sir and young lady." The young man does as he's told. When Jack let's go of his finger, he instantly starts rubbing it. "You better get on your crotch rocket and leave before my friends and I get really mad." Jack looks towards Pete "He doesn't have the patience I have." The young man turns on his heels and runs to his bike. The four young men leave, yelling as they go "You're both crazy!" Pete turns to Jack smiling "Do they think they're telling us something we don't already know?" Jack looks at Pete "You really don't have a gun under there do you?" Sara is looking on, curiously. Pete pulls out a comb "No, just want to look good." He starts combing his hair. Jack says, "Well it's going to take a lot more then that comb to do that." Pete laughs "Ha, ha, ha and did you put a man's finger in a pickle jar?" Jack smiles "No, but it sounded good didn't it." They all laugh and then they are all on the road again, already forgetting about the "incident" that just occurred. They were on a mission, enjoying each other's' company.

After riding for some time, they pull into a motel. They park their bikes and all walk in together. By this time, "Black Widow" doesn't smell nearly as bad. Thank goodness. A short man walks to the counter as they enter the lobby. He has dark hair and a foreign accent; he turns to them and smiles "May I help you?" Pete answers for the three of them "Yes, sir. We would like three rooms please." The man just stares at them for a minute. Sara jumps in wondering if the old man heard Pete, "Is there something wrong?" The little man looks up at Sara and says "You are the "hero's" everyone is talking about. It is an honor for you to stay with us. We have our three best rooms ready for you, hoping you would stop here. Rooms 7, 8 and 9." He turns and hands them the room keys. "Please, if there is anything we can do for you, let us know." The old man is smiling from ear to ear, Sara replies "Thank you so much. You are so kind." Jack never saying word, just shakes his head and turns towards the door to leave. Once outside the office, Jack turns to Sara and says "Sara, you are..." before he can say another word, she cuts him off "What Jack?! What am I? Am I, a.) fantastic b.) wonderful, or c.) beautiful?" She smiles, hoping to de-escalate the situation some. She can tell Jack is a little irritated. Jack just shakes his head and says, "D Sara, all the above." Sara looks at Pete and says, "I knew he loved me." She winks at both of them. Jack says (still shaking his head) "You two try and get a good night's rest. Tomorrow is the big day." They all head into their rooms. Jack, knowing he could not sleep with so much going on in his head, goes out for a walk.

There is a small garden with a park bench right outside their rooms. He sits there, just looking up at the stars. All of a sudden, he hears a voice behind him "Beautiful night isn't it? You can't sleep either, huh?" It's Sara. "I can't stop thinking about Dan." Jack replied. "We had the nicest ride and we owe it all to him. How do we thank him?" Jack looks up as Sara approached the bench in the garden. "Don't worry Jack, he knows. But can you tell me something?" She sits down beside Jack, "What's that?" Jack asks Sara. "Did he ever tell you why he wanted to be put into the Gulf?" Sara looks into Jacks eyes as he responds "Well, I guess Dan's mother loved the Gulf. She loved to sit and watch the sunset in the evenings. She always wanted to go out on a boat but Dan's parents did not have a lot money. Dan's father was a very hard worker, so all of the overtime he worked, he would put that money away. Then for their 15th wedding anniversary, he was able to get two tickets on a boat, just a ride through the Gulf for an evening (dinner included). Dan's mother was thrilled. Any ways, no one knows what happened for sure, but the boat capsized and no one from the boat was ever found. Dan said this was his way of being buried with his parents." Jack turns to Sara, a tear running down her cheek. He takes his thumb and wipes it away, pulls her close and kisses her on the forehead. "Jack, you are a very special friend. Dan thought a lot of you." Sara whispers against his chest. "He saved my life once. I should be the one gone, not him." Jack replied. "Everything happens for a reason, Jack. I'm glad you're here." Sara looks up at him now. "Do you think I'll ever get all this stuff out of my head?" He glances down at her, "I don't know but if you let me, I would love to try." They stare at each other, not saying a word, then they kiss. Jack stops suddenly and holds his head sideways like he is listening to something. He looks at her "Do you hear that?" "Hear what Jack?" Sara is just watching him, confused. He walks a few steps over to her trike; he hits a few buttons and the song "Please Forgive Me" starts playing. Jack says "Their playing our song." Sara looks at him and smiles "We have a song?" With an English accent, Jack replies "Of course we do silly. May I have this dance?" Sara, still smiling goes into Jacks arms. "Jack, you are so romantic, crazy but romantic. That's what I love about you." They start to dance.

The next morning, Pete is the first one up and out of his room. He stands outside his room, stretching from the nice sleep he got the night before. He walks over to Sara's door and knocks. He yells to her "Sara let's get moving. I think it would be nice if we all had breakfast first." There's no response, he knocks again and yells "Hey Sara, you up?" Still nothing. So, Pete walks away talking to himself "Oh great, we will see her around noon." Then he goes and knocks on Jack's door. "Hey Jack, can we go get something to eat? I think Sara is going to be a little while." The door opens and there stands Sara, wearing Jack's t-shirt. "Good morning Pete. Looks like we are going to have another beautiful day." She smiles, Pete just stands there as if he were in shock. Sara goes on "Pete, would you mind going and getting us all some coffee? I know Jack is going to need his large black coffee this morning. That poor man is just exhausted, you know from the trip and all." Pete looks at her "Yeah sure, I will go get coffee." Sara smiles "Thank you Pete. You are so sweet." Then she shuts the door. Pete turns and walks away, talking to himself again "... exhausted from the trip and all. That poor man." He shakes his head and chuckles. After they all had breakfast Jack says "Ok, we have put this off long enough. Let's get started." Jack goes and get the urn and they all walk towards the shoreline. Jack turns to Pete and Sara "This is it. Anyone want to say anything?" Pete looks at the urn "Dan, you are one of the bravest men I ever knew. One of the best friends I ever had, and will be missed more than you will ever know." Sara then looks at Jack "May I?" Jack hands her the urn and takes the top off. Sara walks out into the water until it's just above her knees. She slowly turns the urn upside down and watches the ash's fall into the water. Tears rolling down her face. When it's empty, she turns to walk back towards Jack and Pete, who are standing at attention and saluting Dan. As Sara reaches Jack and Pete, she has a blank look on her face. "What's wrong" Jack asks her. She just points behind them and says "Look!" Jack and Pete turn to see what looked like hundreds of people standing there. Some with American flags, some with POW/MIA flags and some with signs saying "Our Vets, All Vets, and Our Hero's" . The three look at one another, tears falling down each of the ir faces, they hug. "Dan would have never expected this." Pete says to them. "No" Jack says, "he wouldn't have expected it, but he did deserve it."

To all of our hero's: GOD BLESS and THANK YOU!

Printed in the United States
by Baker & Taylor Publisher Services